SLATCOFF AN
Publishi

www.SLATCOFF.com

Remember your ancestors.

A CHRISTMAS STORY

The Curse of
No Christmas Kołaczki

by
THOMAS SLATCOFF

The Curse of No Christmas Kołaczki 2021-12 SSF2
The Curse of No Christmas Kołaczki Hardcover 2022-11 SSF2

Description

Tomasz, the baby of the family, knew more than his three older brothers about the old country curse No Christmas Kołaczki (koh-WAHTCH-kee). So, at the age of seven years, the family baby demanded a grave responsibility for himself. He authorized himself to solve the mystery of the family's missing Christmas Kołaczki to save his family and himself from the old country curse.

About the Author

Thomas Slatcoff returned to private business after serving twenty-three years in federal law enforcement and retired as a senior criminal investigator.

Thomas has authored three novels: *Operation Red X*, his debut novel, *Atrocity in the Nave*, *The Respondent: A Person of Interest*, and a short story, *The Respondent: A Person Bewitched*, a prelude to *The Respondent: A Person of Interest*.

He uses his diverse experiences, knowledge, and observations from private business, global government service, federal law enforcement, public safety, and life to create literary works to entertain, inform, and inspire. Thomas spends his time in Florida and Pennsylvania and traveling.

Visit SLATCOFF.com for more about Thomas and SLATCOFF AND COMPANY.

Enjoy the read! Stay in touch.

Twitter
THOMASSLATCOFFBOOKS@SLATCOFFANDCO

Facebook
SLATCOFFANDCOMPANYLLC@SLATCOFFANDCOMPANY

LinkedIn
THOMAS SLATCOFF

Copy Editor

Anne-Marie Rutella

Cover Art

Cover Illustration
@Andreus / depositphotos.com

Cover Design
Beetiful (beetifulbookcovers.com)

The Curse of No Christmas Kołaczki is a work of fiction.

The names, characters, and events in the short story are the product of the author's imagination. Therefore, they are used fictitiously and not intended as accurate representations of real incidents or people, living or dead.

The places, cities, towns, organizations, and entities are used fictitiously and not intended as accurate representations of real places, cities, towns, organizations, and entities or anyone, in any manner, associated with the same.

Copyright © 2021 by
SLATCOFF AND COMPANY LLC

All rights reserved.

In accordance with the U.S. Copyright Act of 1976, the scanning, uploading, and electronic sharing of any part of this book without the permission of the publisher is unlawful piracy and theft of the author's intellectual property. If you would like to use material from the book, other than for review purposes, please obtain prior written permission by contacting the publisher at Contact@Slatcoff.com.

Thank you for the support of the publisher's rights.

Published by:

Florida, USA
Contact@Slatcoff.com
www.Slatcoff.com

First Print Edition: December 2021
The Curse of No Christmas Kołaczki Hardcover 2022-10
ISBN- 978-0-9971506-7-4

Acknowledgments

Thank you to those who continue to support me in my literary journey.

Mary, Samantha, Lauren, Bethany

Your support and enthusiasm motivates me.

Your love for me and belief in me inspires me.

Your belief that I have something to offer others flatters me.

Love you.

A Christmas Short Story

from the imagination of
Grandpa from Pittsburgh

for my grandsons

Jacob Michael Martinko
and
John Thomas Martinko

Remember your ancestors.

DAWNO DAWNO TEMU

there was a little boy named Tomasz, the last of four children, all boys. He was the family baby and often referred to as the baby of the family, baby brother, or the little boy. He was a second-generation, natural-born citizen of the United States of America. He was born in Windber, a coal town in the Allegheny Mountains, in southwestern Pennsylvania, and raised in the coal mining patch town Mine 40.

The four boys were born to loving and doting parents. Their father was of Bulgarian descent and their mother was of Polish descent. Both parents were first-generation, natural-born U.S. citizens. The proud parents raised their four boys in the lower half of a four-room, former company house that the parents had purchased at some point in the 1950s or 1960s.

When Tomasz was seven years old, he demanded for himself a grave responsibility–to save his family from the old country curse of No Christmas Kołaczki.

2. *IT ALL BEGAN*

in the late nineteenth century, atop the Alleghany Mountains, in an area that held the bituminous rich coalfields in southwestern Pennsylvania. Coalfields that stretched throughout Somerset County and farther north, east, and west into Pennsylvania, and south into the border state of West Virginia.

Northeastern Somerset County farmland was the surveyed location for a coal-mining town settled in 1897 and quickly became a bustling town by the 1900s. It was named Windber, a derivative of the surname of two brothers, both coal barons from the City of Brotherly Love, Philadelphia, Pennsylvania. However, coal-town gossip opined the coal baron brothers never stepped a foot in Windber.

The two coal baron brothers and a third co-owner formed a nineteenth-century corporation that the immigrant workfource dubbed The Company. It was The Company who built Windber and owned it.

For the good of The Company and its owners, The Company planned, built, and controlled many coal-mining patch towns on the outskirts of Windber, throughout Somerset County, and elsewhere in the bituminous coal region. The Company used the number of the mine opening for the patch town name. Thus, for example, one of The Company-built patch towns was Mine 40.

Mine 40, built to represent a model coal mining operation, was built with amenities in a hollow on the outskirts of Windber. Amenities were a big deal at that time, and the

Mine 40 amenities included: company wood-built houses with indoor plumbing, a company store, a company hotel with a bar, and all the buildings and latest equipment of the time necessary for a smooth-running, coal mining operation.

The Company built the houses with three different cookie-cutter models. The houses were laid out in a grid formation, sprawled northeastward away from the mine opening. They followed the land's upward slope and were built for the coal miners to rent. The patch town layout facilitated the coal miners to walk to work.

The mine opening, office building, and the miners' washhouse were all situated at the bottom of the patch town, near the creek.

The Company recruited a European blue-collar labor force that traveled the rough sea crossing and arrived as an ethnically diverse pool of able-bodied men. Some with and some without families. The immigrant workers settled among *their kind*, to use the vernacular. The coal town quickly became ethnically segregated into enclaves of Magyars (Hungarians), Carpatho-Russians, Poles, Slavs, Slovaks, and Italians. The patch town Mine 40 blended the Eastern European ethnic groups and a few Mexican families among the five streets.

The Company managed the diverse immigrant labor force with voluntary servitude, which was the perceived relationship between the immigrant coal miners and The Company's business model. A business model that was designed with production pay for labor and diverse income streams for The Company.

Production pay for labor was a creative system of servitude masked by scant employee wages paid for the tonnage of coal the immigrant coal miner harvested. The miners continually disputed The Company's tonnage numbers due to questionable weighing tactics by the weighmasters who were company men. If the coal miner labored to set posts, blast rock, or cleared stone to get to the coal for their underground shift, they did not make any money that day. Such labor efforts and results were not considered tonnage. However, their related work supplies were credited to their company store book.

Two examples of The Company's diverse streams of income included:

The property rental of company houses—the lower or upper half of a double house The Company built and rented to the immigrant coal miners. The Company deducted the monthly rent payment directly from the coal miner's gross pay.

The Company's stores were where the immigrant employees were required to shop exclusively, using a store credit book. The immigrant miners shopped at The Company's patch town stores or The Company's big store in Windber.

The miners had to buy all their work and personal goods at The Company stores. The stores credited the goods to the coal miner's store credit book and deducted the payments directly from the immigrant coal miner's gross pay. When the Company man, or boss, as the immigrant coal miners called them, found out an immigrant coal miner bought something at a location other than The Company stores, the boss charged that miner's store book the amount the item or items cost at The Company store. The Company's business model confused the definitions of authorized credit and forced indebtedness.

So it was on payday that the immigrant coal miner received, as pay for work, the balance the weighmaster maintained weekly with suspicious accounting of the tonnage mined, multiplied by the rate per tonnage, minus The Company store book credits. So, were there coal miners in the negative? Yes. Quite often.

There was no denying it. Immigrant coal miners were on the low end of the economic scale. As stated in the vernacular of the patch town inhabitants, "Immigrant coal miners don't have a pot to piss in."

Or as Tennessee Ernie Ford sang in his top hit song "Sixteen Tons"

> *"You load sixteen tons, what do you get?*
> *Another day older and deeper in debt.*
> *St. Peter, don't you call me 'cause I can't go,*
> *I owe my soul to the company store."*

But immigrant coal miners had dreams. And their dreams were not dissolved by the harsh working conditions or by the distance and time away from their families back in the old country. The immigrants' difficulties did not deter the strong-minded, strong-backed, proud coal miners from making a better life for their families. Both the family that journeyed with them to the new country and the family they left behind in the old country but whom the miners continued to care for.

The immigrant coal miners never admitted they were homesick for the old country. Their egos negated self-pity. Though the new and the old countries were always in a state of comparison, the reasons remained elusive.

There was a beer garden on every corner, which the youth believed was the reason why the proud adult immigrants were a happy lot. They were pleased as punch from the everyday indulgences at one of the many corner bars, ethnic social clubs, war veterans clubs, home delivery of beer, or a meager clubhouse in the back alleys used for gambling by card playing. All the locations maintained alcohol and smokes to facilitate high spirits that combated the harsh realities of life in the new country.

There was an ethnic church on every corner in the ethnic enclaves of the coal town. The churches provided cohesion for the diverse ethnic groups in the new country, where Mass was in their language, with their people, and most often, said by a priest who came to the bustling coal town from their old country. Built by, and so exclusive to a single ethnic group, the churches were referred to by the ethnicity of the parishioners—the Polish church, the Hungarian church, the Italian church, and so on.

The church was their refuge from the new country's unknown, different, and harsh realities for the immigrants. The four walls of the church were like being within the borders of the old country—all things done there as done in the old country. The place where the immigrants carried out their traditions and celebrated holidays, especially Christmas.

The subsequent natural-born generations, those born on the soil of the United States of America, which made them instant citizens of the new country, shared the traits of their immigrant ancestors—a strong mind and a strong back. The first-generation immigrants were proud happy people, too. Many immigrant offspring followed their foreign-speaking parents into the underground work sites—some as young as fourteen.

3. CHANGES CAME TO THE MOUNTAINS

in the mid-twentieth century. One major event was the 1958 layoffs that hit the bituminous coalfields because of the decline in the demand for coal. As a result, many first- and second-generation ethnic coal miners found themselves without work and faced the decision of migrating for employment, as had their ancestors.

The Company sold their rental houses. This was the case with house number 934, the lower half of a former company house. It was built in the early 1900s by The Company and situated on Wissinger Road in patch town Mine 40. It was a typical cookie-cutter patch town design—a four-room company house with a single cellar bathroom of the late nineteenth-century fashion.

The former house 934 succumbed to change. The house had the rear porch enclosed and a modern enclosed bathroom with a tub was added off the first-floor kitchen. The balance of the porch was outfitted to a small fifth room referred to as the porch. Likewise, as time went on, the kitchen was remodeled, too.

A unique characteristic of the patch towns was that family members lived near one another. House number 936, the upper half of 934, was also a four-room company house. It was once home to Tomasz's grandfather on his father's side who, as a Bulgarian immigrant coal miner, rented the house from The Company to provide shelter for his family. And it was once the home of Tomasz's uncle Camden, his father's brother. A little farther up the street, number 940 was the home of Tomasz's mother's sister, Halina. A half of house on First Street was home to Tomasz's Uncle Yoan, another of father's brothers.

4. MID-1960s

Christmastime in the hollow was once again upon the people of the ethnically diverse, predominately Catholic, rural patch town on the outskirts of the now semi bustling coal town. The Christian immigrant coal miners of various denominations all celebrated Christmas with jubilation.

In the hollow, on Wissinger Road, house 934 was home to a happy family of six. The father, a first-generation U.S. citizen by birth and a laid-off coal miner by supply and demand, started working as a miner at the age of fourteen and worked for production rates, which were fifty cents a ton. He was a veteran of World War II and the Korean Conflict and was now a delivery truck driver. The mother was a housewife and always worked with a smile. She had never been laid off and never missed a workday, but would soon find it necessary to work outside the home as a retail clerk. All four children, all boys with Polish given names, from oldest to youngest—Piotr, Antoni, Zeffi, and Tomasz—lived a carefree life because of parental doting. Altogether, they were the happy half dozen.

Tomasz and his family celebrated Christmas from the perspective of the Eastern Rite Byzantine Catholics with the traditions and customs their Eastern European ancestors brought with them when they crossed the Atlantic Ocean. Traditions and customs for which subsequent generations showed the same jubilation. Traditions and customs Father and Mother showed their four boys through their high-spirited holiday actions.

Christmas was Tomasz's favorite religious holiday. First, of course, the spiritual birth of Baby Jesus, God's only son, was humbly celebrated by the family. So, as a tradition, it was paramount that the family went to the midnight liturgy and celebrated amid the grandeur of the festive decorations at St. Mary's Byzantine Greek Catholic Church. Before the midnight liturgy, caroling in English and Old Church Slavonic was a high point Tomasz enjoyed with his mother.

Tomasz was also amid the Christmas grandeur at home and throughout the community. Christmas decorations. Ethnic Christmas foods. Family gatherings. Memories shared. Memories made. The family christmas traditions. Caroling during the public-school day. The town's war veterans' clubs, the American Legion and the Veterans of Foreign Wars, hosted Christmas parties for the youth with hot chocolate, cookies, and Christmas movies. There was also a visit from Santa Claus. For a verbal share of their Christmas list, Santa gave the children the famous coal town white Christmas treat bag filled with a box of animal cookies, a long thick candy cane, the hard round flavored candy with a hole in the middle, a small box of chocolate-covered cherries, and a popcorn ball. A Christmas activity and treats that made memories.

For Tomasz, his Christmas memory of memories was the ethnic Christmas home-baked goods. Tomasz had an enormous sweet tooth. Perhaps an inherited sugar gene. Tomasz did not know. Tomasz did not care. For Tomasz, Christmas equated ethnic home-baked goods. Midnight liturgy was paramount. Presents, of course. There was a presents list carefully checked more than twice. The boy's Christmas lists were annotated with their favorite ethnic home-baked goods. On Tomasz's list, the cookies were capitalized, underlined, highlighted, and circled. His favorite was the golden jubilee with white icing. A simple icing made from water, powdered sugar, and a hint of vanilla, atop a plain dough cookie mixed with small, crushed walnuts. Christmas Kołaczki was his second favorite.

5. *SEVEN DAYS TO CHRISTMAS*

The Christmas season was in full swing, in the half of the house, in all the hollow, and in the coal town. The scene was with superabundant exterior house decoration throughout the coal mine patch towns and in the coal town.

Mother started her traditional Christmas baking three days prior. She started from her Polish roots, and the first cookie she baked was the Christmas Kołaczki. A cookie the entire family liked and ate by the handful. Depending on the size of the hand based on age, a handful counted three to eight cookies per grab on average. So, as the family's baby, poor little Tomasz had the most petite hands, which left him holding only three cookies at a grab. Sometimes four, if he squeezed tight enough. If he squeezed too tight, Tomasz changed the entire composition of the Christmas Kołaczki. At times, this resulted from his excitement for the two-bite Christmas cookie.

These family dynamics did not deter Tomasz's Christmas cookie savor. Tomasz had a Christmas cookie consumption strategy based on speed over time. A formula that did not require any knowledge of algebra, geometry, or any of the sciences—biology, chemistry, or physics. Big or small hands did not matter. It merely required tenacity. He was not bashful about cheering himself on to an ethnic Christmas home-baked goods bliss. His inner motivational cheer—*Go, tenacious Tomasz. Eat those cookies.*

Mother started her Christmas baking with the Christmas Kołaczki because it was the most time-consuming of the dozens of cookies she made. The dough was time-consuming to prepare. That was the first step. In the second step, Mother pinched off a small ball and rolled it out with her aged rolling pin to a thickness measured by her touch of experience. Then she cut the rolled dough into roughly three-inch squares. Mother cut the dough with a fancy wheeled cutting implement that made a decorative edge to the dough, to the baked cookie. Each square was filled with a tablespoon of filling, no more, no less. Prominent was Mother's proprietary homemade walnut filling, the recipe from the infamous green cookbook the *Anniversary Slovak-American Cook Book*. It, too, had to be prepared and embellished with Mother's secret ingredients. She also used the prepared Baker jar filling and only Baker as she reminded Father the many times he left the house to do the Christmas baking shopping. Baker's filling flavors were poppy seed, apricot, pineapple, and sometimes cherry. The flavor of the filling depended on what The Company's big store stocked or what Father found on sale at various grocery stores along his delivery routes throughout Somerset County. With Mother's precise dollop of filling placed on the dough, two of the opposite four corners of the squares were folded over and pinched. The kołaczki was baked to a golden brown and then left to cool. Once cooled, Mother packed them into the black roaster pan and two old tin cans depending on the size of the yield. One piece of erratically torn wax paper separated the layers. The containers were placed either on the attic steps or atop Mother's wooden hope chest in her and Father's bedroom, the back bedroom. The bedroom with a wooden door to access the attic.

6. THE RESPONSIBILITY OF BABY BROTHER

So, it was to reason, that during one of the baby's childhood Christmases—his seventh Christmas to be exact—Tomasz knew first and foremost that he had to be the family member to solve the mystery of the missing Christmas Kołaczki and present the likely harsh reality. The culprit of the mystery of the missing Christmas Kołaczki was most likely someone among the happy half dozen. A family member was Tomasz's hunch.

Tomasz knew more than his three older brothers about the old country curse No Christmas Kołaczki. Tomasz spent more than a few sleepless nights after being out with his father on the Wissinger Road summertime front porch socials.

During some of the front porch socials, the baby heard firsthand the horrid stories about the old country curse as the adults exchanged memories and stories. These were descriptive exchanges about someone responsible for a Christmas void of Christmas Kołaczki and the someone accountable for their family's affliction with the curse No Christmas Kołaczki.

The sleepless nights came from the echo of the facts twirling in Tomasz's mind that entire families perished to extinction, full bloodlines. They died from the curse No Christmas Kołaczki. A curse a family risked when Christmas Kołaczki went missing pre-midnight liturgy. During the Great Philip's Fast. Before the celebration of the birth of Baby Jesus. Before Christmas Day. And heaven forbid if a family member ate any Christmas Kołaczki on the Byzantine Feast of Saint Nicholas, which had its unique cookie.

Memorable to Tomasz was when one of the porch social members started to speak about eating Christmas Kołaczki on the Byzantine Feast of Saint Nicholas, which made the porch silent. All the adults stopped talking and lowered their heads in unison. The entire patch town Mine 40 went quiet, so it seemed. The silence spooked Tomasz, and he cuddled to his father for security. Even the Hungarian, a tall, burly, baritone-sounding, profanity-using, scary-looking porch social adult, with the pungent odor of alcohol, teared up on one occasion of remembering the curse.

Tomasz had trembled when he thought, *Yes, any missing Christmas Kołaczki is indeed a grave matter of concern.*

Now Tomasz tugged up his ironed, creased, husky-sized pants. He tucked his hand-me-down ironed T-shirt into his pants and tightened his frayed black leather belt a hole or two more. He combed his hair with a part to the left and a pompadour to the right. He cleaned his broken, white-taped, black-rimmed glasses. The glass lenses were buffed to a sheen. Finally, he threw his shoulders back, so he stood tall in his pudgy Polish frame. All was intended to present a mature demeanor, so the other five family members would take the baby seriously—a challenge Tomasz had to manage for the family to survive.

A reckless family member was a rare occurrence for the disciplined, happy, fun-loving Polish and Bulgarian ethnically blended home. But, as troubling as it was, it appeared this Christmas, during the Great Philip's Fast, someone—more than likely one of the other five of the half dozen—stepped away from their strong Byzantine Eastern Catholic religious principles. Someone compromised their character. Someone abandoned their integrity. Someone placed self before family. Someone ate Christmas Kołaczki, and that someone did it before Christmas. Before the end of midnight liturgy. Someone committed a no-no, a big no-no. The fine for the crime was not merely a lump of coal but the possibility of a horrid outcome—the old country curse levied on the entire family. The whole half dozen cursed with Christmas void of Christmas Kołaczki. No Christmas Kołaczki for possibly years.

Tomasz thought, *Even me. I'm a member of the family. I know I didn't eat any of the Kołaczki, but I'm going down with the family unless I can finger the Kołaczki thief.*

I know family solidarity forgives many things. And that family forgiveness is very charitable. However, a Christmas Kołaczki thief? A thief among the happy half dozen. The family solidarity stands a test with this event. And this event, this crime, needs a resolution expeditiously.

Save the Christmas Kołaczki or suffer a Christmas void of Christmas Kołaczki.

And to quote the members of the Wissinger Road summertime front porch socials, "The old country curse of No Christmas Kołaczki, be damned."

Tomasz's thoughts made him tremble at the notion of a Christmas void of Christmas Kołaczki. The harsh reality—a single Christmas void of Christmas Kołaczki—could fester a curse for years to come of No Christmas Kołaczki. It was a curse that had crossed the vast Atlantic Ocean with the immigrant coal miners and, like Tomasz's ancestors, it also survived the long, harsh sea crossing. The old country curse No Christmas Kołaczki was in the new country, and it was real. A situation Tomasz cared not to risk

7. THE CHRISTMAS KOŁACZKI FACTS

In his mind, and like a meticulous detective, Tomasz retraced the events of this year's Christmas Kołaczki as he knew them.

15 December, Thursday

All the Christmas Kołaczki were intact—baked, packed, and placed on the wooden hope chest in the back bedroom. I knew this because when I came home from school on Thursday afternoon, Mother asked me to take the tins and black roaster and place them on the wooden hope chest. In front of me, the last thing Mother did was close the tin tops tight. As Mother placed the respective lids on the containers, I saw the yield filled all three.

17 December, Saturday

At breakfast, I witnessed Mother announce the Christmas Kołaczki were missing. She had warned everyone not to eat any Christmas Kołaczki or cookies except the broken or burnt ones left on the kitchen counter after the day's baking.

I also observed a fretful mother. Rarely did Mother fret. But, on that Saturday, Mother's face showed worry over the missing Christmas Kołaczki.

Perhaps fear of a possible Christmas void of Christmas Kołaczki, though she did not say anything about the possible impending curse. That was Mother. She never projected her problems or worries onto others.

Tomasz paused and realized, *That's not a whole lot to go on.*

8. CHRISTMAS EVE AT THE FIRST STAR

The family commenced their Christmas Eve meal per the tradition of the sight of the first star. When finished, everyone went a different way. Mother started to prepare the Christmas meal—potato salad sprinkled with paprika, macaroni salad sprinkled with paprika, deviled eggs sprinkled with paprika, golabki cooked with sauerkraut in a clear broth with a touch of paprika. Father, too. He began the long slow boil of the ham and the kielbasa. He also made his famed pickled red beets with onions and hard-boiled eggs. All the courses were ethnic holiday food traditions that filled the house with a procession of holiday aromas.

The somber Tomasz climbed the stairs from the kitchen to the second floor, unrecognized. At the top landing, he paused and leaned against the wood-paneled shared wall between the lower half and upper half of the former company house. The coal-fired gravity heat lofted from the small single upstairs register. The warmth warmed Tomasz's body but did nothing for his frigid spirit.

Tomasz thought, *Did I just witness the last family hustle and bustle for Christmas preparation? The last Christmas for the family? I have no leads. None!*

Tomasz was no closer to solving the case of the missing Christmas Kołaczki on Christmas Eve than he was last Saturday when his mother mentioned it. The lore of the curse required the perpetrator to be apprehended and dealt with before the start of the midnight liturgy, before Christmas Day. That was the only way to repel the curse.

Emotions bubbled within Tomasz. A tear popped from his blue eye and rolled down his chubby Polish cheek and onto the carpeted floor. He removed his black-rimmed glasses with his left hand and used his right hand to retrieve a neatly folded and ironed white handkerchief. He flicked his wrist to open the cloth and wiped his eyes and cheek to recompose himself quickly. Next, he positioned his glasses on his face, refolded the handkerchief per the ironed creases, and returned it to his right rear pocket. He knew he had work to do, so he tugged up his husky-sized blue jeans. But first, he had to take a nap, so that he would be rested for the midnight liturgy. The nap was at the command of Mother.

9. *MIDNIGHT DIVINE LITURGY*

The four boys were ready. All dressed in their Christmas best with their hair combed and shoes shined. They were seated on the living room couch like little soldiers, and surprisingly, they sat at attention. Father might have had a word with them. Or, in the glow of the multicolored lighted Christmas tree, thoughts danced in their heads of what presents they might receive from good old Santa Claus.

Father was seated in his chair at the kitchen table. He smoked a cigarette and sipped his coffee. He looked as he always did, deep in thought as he rubbed the palms of his hands together. Father, too, was dressed in his Christmas best—a suit, white shirt, complementing tie, and shined shoes. His flattop-style hair did not require combing.

Then Mother made her entrance into the kitchen. The sweet bouquet of her perfume trailed her and then loitered. It was rare to see Mother gussied up except for Sunday church or infrequent special occasions. For the church holidays, Christmas and Easter, she went a bit extra and had her hair done at the beauty salon in the coal town. For Christmas, she wore her pearls. One strand in the medium-length style. A rare, rare occurrence for a demure, humble lady.

With everyone ready, the happy half dozen was off to St. Mary's Byzantine Greek Catholic Church in Windber.

After Father parked in the church parking lot, the two older brothers skipped off to serve as altar boys with the hope of receiving the usual generous altar boy Christmas gift, a whole box of milk chocolate-covered cherries—the two-layer box. The rest of the family made their way to the front of the church. They entered and moved through the European-tiled vestibule, which was decorated with Christmas trees and wreaths. They paraded down the right-side aisle and took their usual pew on the right-hand side, six rows back so that Tomasz could see everything.

Simple Christmas decorations were on display. A dozen live Christmas trees were positioned about the front of the church and altar, with tiny white lights that twinkled. A wreath was arranged midway up all the long stained-glass windows, with medium-sized multicolored lights aglow. A white plastic seven-candle candelabra was placed one per window seal, with red lights glowing. A large manger scene took the place of the right-hand side altar and included a Magi star high up the wall. Red and white poinsettias decorated the main altar. The aroma of Christmas filled the church.

Home from divine liturgy, everyone hurried and changed from their church clothes. Finally, the family assembled at the kitchen table for the traditional after-Christmas midnight liturgy meal, which now included meat, unlike the Christmas Eve meal. The time was 2:00 a.m., but everyone was eating from all the dishes Mother and Father had prepared. The after-midnight liturgy meal was a Christmas tradition of unknown origins.

After enjoying the food and cleaning the kitchen, the family retired from a long day. However, the excitement of opening presents would have four of the half dozen up shortly after sunrise.

10. A VISION OF THE CURSE

Tomasz did not encounter a vision of the curse. Until now, he only experienced the worry of not solving the mystery of the missing Christmas Kołaczki. This brought Tomasz tears of failure. A big task that gave Tomasz the persistent echo in his head, *"What else could I do?"*

Tomasz snuggled into his tear-dampened pillow. Slowly, he drifted off to dreamland, but there were no visions of sugarplums dancing in his head. There was no army of toy soldiers to protect the family from the curse. Nutcrackers were not standing guard over the family to keep evil spirits and danger away. There were only baby tears from the family baby, brought on by the thoughts of an impending curse. Possibly a lifetime curse on the entire family. Grown-up thoughts of the baby's failure. And the echo in his head, *what else could I do?* An echo that finally lulled Tomasz to sleep and to dream…

Tomasz turned left and entered the back bedroom. He observed—the Kołaczki tins were in place; the lids were secure; likewise, the black roaster. However, he observed crumbs on the surface of the wooden hope chest.

The self-proclaimed family's private eye looked about to ensure no one was around. Then, alone, he slowly walked to the hope chest for a closer examination of the dubious crumbs. He picked up a medium-sized crumb, raised it to his nose, and carefully discerned its scent.

Tomasz sounded, "Hmm."

He opened his lips and clenched his teeth to expose his gums. When he rubbed the crumb on his gums, he instantly experienced a sugar rush from immediately absorbing the high-grade sweet compound of processed white sugar, honey, and walnuts into his body. Though an inexperienced youth, he had developed eating experience beyond his years. He shook his head in the affirmative. It was a decisive match.

Tomasz thought slowly and deliberately, *It's a high-grade Kołaczki crumb, nut-filled, of this year's vintage, based on my comparison of tasting some of the broken and burnt ones allowed by the holiday baking tradition and Mother's okay.*

He inspected the floor. Similar bits were on the rug and formed a line.

Staring at the crumb line, Tomasz thought, *I finally got a lead?*

He followed the trail of crumbs. It led to the wooden attic door and then disappeared. Without hesitation, Tomasz put his ear to the door. He listened but heard nothing. He reached out, took hold of the doorknob, gently twisted it until he heard the latch release, and then slowly pulled the door open. He continued to peer into the darkness of a makeshift closet as the door opened bit by bit. There was no one there. He opened the door wider for natural light to aid his investigation. The light confirmed no one was there.

Tomasz looked to the floor and continued to follow the Kołaczki crumb trail. Near the bottom step was a pile of crumbs. The crumbs were situated neatly and orderly as if someone had brushed them into a pile for pickup with a damp paper towel. He flicked the attic light on and examined the stairs. He saw nothing, no one. It was apparent the trail ended at the bottom landing of the attic steps. There was the appearance that someone had sat there and had eaten the Christmas Kołaczki.

Tomasz stood at the bottom of the attic steps in thought, *Is this the Kołaczki thief's hideout? Is this the place where the crime ended? Is this where the thief disposed of the spoils of his crime—the Christmas Kołaczki? Is this the thief's haunt? Did the Kołaczki thief maintain a haunt right under my nose?*

After a moment, Tomasz turned the attic light off, tugged up his pants, walked back into the bedroom from the alleged Kołaczki thief's hideout, and closed the door behind him. He noted that the alarm clock on the bedside table showed 6:30. Then, he walked to the larger of the two tins and twisted it to position it to a mark. Tomasz's investigative strategy—if someone handled the tin the mark would be moved and give a window of time someone was in the room. Something necessary for interrogations later.

As Tomasz walked out of the back bedroom, he thought, *I am running out of time. I must do something. For the love of Baby Jesus, it's Christmas Eve.*

From the back bedroom, Tomasz went into the front bedroom. At the edge of the bed, he sat deep in thought for his next investigative move. He was brought back from deep thought by the sound of someone rushing up the stairs. He thought it was one of his brothers coming into the bedroom to get their gloves or hat or whatever for sled riding. He did not move.

The footsteps hit the top landing and swiftly flowed into the back bedroom. A tin top popped like the sound of Father's government-issued Model 1911 .45 ACP that he had brought home from the battlefields of World War II and only fired on New Year's Day in celebration. Then came the rustle of the wax paper. Finally, the last sound, the struggle of the tin top being popped back on the tin.

Tomasz's eyes opened wide. His hands started to shake, and he slowly rose from the bed. He stood for a moment. His hands were still shaking, so he took a deep breath to calm himself. He exhaled. Baby brother knew what he had to do. Carefully, he walked to the front bedroom door. He started to inch through to the top landing. He had to see who was in the back bedroom. The someone Tomasz had to apprehend to end this.

Again, Tomasz thought, *Was this the someone responsible for the missing Christmas Kołaczki? Was this a break in the investigation to save the family from the old country curse, No Christmas Kołaczki?*

Tomasz was about to step entirely through the front bedroom doorway when Piotr, Tomasz's oldest brother, ran into him. The velocity of the oldest brother's flight from his illegal Christmas Kołaczki take knocked Tomasz back into the front bedroom and onto the bed next to the closet. The Kołaczki the oldest brother had wrapped in wax paper flew into the air. They landed scattered on the bedroom floor, the beds, and two landed on Tomasz's chest.

Piotr filled with rage. His eyes did not twinkle like St. Nicholas. His brother's eyes turned colors—one went red, the other went green. His Christmas-colored eyes discharged red-and-green flames in the direction of Tomasz.

Piotr shouted, "You made me drop my Christmas Kołaczki."

Tomasz froze on the bed. He lay paralyzed by the vision of his oldest brother's flaming red-and-green eyes. He was paralyzed by the remembrance of the words of the adults from the Wissinger Road summertime front porch socials. With the demonic qualities, Piotr looked and acted as the porch social adults described as someone responsible for missing Christmas Kołaczki. Someone accountable for the curse.

Piotr took two steps and was in front of Tomasz. The eldest brother grabbed the baby brother by his pressed white T-shirt with both hands and what seemed like superhuman strength. In the process, two Kołaczki with cherry filling, one under each of the brother's hands, smashed onto the chest of Tomasz's pressed white T-shirt and left two red marks.

Tomasz felt pain. He looked down and saw the red marks.

"Is that blood?" Tomasz asked himself. "Am I bleeding?"

Tomasz quickly reached up and swabbed one of the red marks with his right-hand pointer finger. Then, he raised the red-tipped finger to his mouth and cautiously tasted the red substance.

Tomasz sighed and then mumbled, "No, only smashed cherry filling from the Kołaczki."

Tomasz worked to remain calm. First, he took a couple of deep breaths. Then, he tried to negotiate with Piotr. Finally, out of desperation, he said to his enraged brother, "Stop, or I am going to tell Mom you're picking on me."

The idle threat only served to elevate the brother's rage. His eyes turned a more intense red and green, and he began to shoot flaming Christmas tree ornaments from his eyes.

Tomasz scrambled. He crawled backward on his elbows and feet. He thrashed his arms about to protect himself from the molten Christmas tree ornaments.

Piotr roared with laughter as he reached out and grabbed his little brother by the legs. Big brother picked baby brother up from the bed and twirled him around in the air. Then, on the sixth rotation, Piotr launched Tomasz into the double sliding closet doors, which went off track on Tomasz's impact. Tomasz came to rest and laid there on the floor.

Big brother turned to the room and collected all the scattered Christmas Kołaczki. He frantically stuffed them into his mouth with both hands. Then he turned and moved back to Tomasz. Kołaczki crumbs fell from his mouth as he knelt over his baby brother and started to choke him.

11. *CHRISTMAS MORNING*

Christmas morning arrived with misadventure afoot in the front bedroom.

Zeffi, Tomasz's brother, broke the day when he shouted, "Tomasz, are you all right? Are you all right?"

Yet another of the brothers, Antoni, sat up in his bed. Groggily, he inquired, "What's going on over there? What's all the noise? I'm trying to sleep over here."

Zeffi saw Tomasz had rolled off the bed and into the closet doors. He moved to the closet side of the bed and looked to the floor. He saw Tomasz was wrestling with a loose stitched crocheted afghan made from green yarn. His baby brother's head poked through a hole in the afghan. His hands also pushed through the afghan, one hole each, and thrashed about in the air. His eyes were closed. Zeffi witnessed that as Tomasz tugged at the afghan, it tightened more around his neck.

Still wanting to sleep more, Antoni moaned, "Tell him to be quiet."

"Help me. Tomasz needs help," shouted a now frantic Zeffi. "He's choking himself with the afghan."

Zeffi rushed to Tomasz's side.

"What do you mean?" Antoni said as he crawled out of his bed and moved to see the plight of his baby brother. When he saw him, he laughed—uncontrolled, deep gut laughter.

Zeffi reached out and shook his baby brother. Then, with sincere concern in his voice, he called out, "Tomasz. Tomasz."

Antoni lurched toward Tomasz and, without hesitation, punched him in the head.

Zeffi jumped back. He looked to Antoni and demanded, "Why did you hit him in the head?"

"I woke him up," Antoni replied. "Look."

Zeffi looked back to Tomasz, whose eyes were wide open now. His hands slowed and then came to rest on the floor. He sat there and repeatedly took deep breaths. The afghan was still around his neck. His hands still poked through.

Zeffi sat back and broke out in laughter. Antoni started to laugh again. Tomasz sat there with his eyes wide open. Dazed, he looked around and rubbed his head on the spot where Antoni hit him. He looked from Zeffi to Antoni, then down to the afghan around his neck. His dream had him in a state of confused caution.

"What is this?" Tomasz asked.

As he tried to control his laughter, Zeffi asked, "What were you dreaming about?"

"I don't know," Tomasz replied as he continued to rub his head. "It was a dream about the missing Christmas

Kołaczki. The curse of No Christmas Kołaczki. A curse from the old country brought to the new country."

Zeffi interrupted, with a tone of no interest in the old country curse, and said, "You rolled off the bed and into the closet doors."

Zeffi continued to laugh at his baby brother.

"What are you talking about?" Antoni asked. "Do you need another punch?"

"A Christmas void of Christmas Kołaczki," Tomasz finished with a somber tone.

Antoni started to move away as he said, "You better put those doors back on the track. That's going to make Dad mad, and it's Christmas."

Starting to control his laughter, Zeffi said, "I think you had too much kielbasa after midnight liturgy. Maybe it was the six deviled eggs, both halves, six whole eggs, a half dozen eggs, with all that paprika at two o'clock in the morning. Maybe it was the pickled red beets and onions eaten with the deviled eggs. Or could it have been the half a pound of potato salad you ate with the browned-off kielbasa rounds? All of that before you went to bed!"

At that moment, Piotr strolled into the front bedroom. His hands cradled a mound of Christmas Kołaczki wrapped in wax paper. One, a walnut filled, hung off his lips like a cigarette. He chewed, and as crumbs fell, he asked, "Would anyone like one?"

Just then, they heard the words for which every Christmas morning they waited.

"Are you boys coming down to open Christmas gifts?" From the bottom of the stairs sounded Father's voice with excitement in it.

The boys were excited now. They knew they could not go downstairs without Mom and Dad on Christmas Day. They could not wake their parents, either. They had to wait for their parents to wake up. They did not know if this was a Christmas tradition or an order.

The brothers—even Tomasz, still dazed, still on the floor, with his head poking through the crocheted afghan, hands the same—looked to each other. Each talked over the other and greeted,

> **"Christos Razdajetsya!**
> **Christ is born!**
>
> **Slave Jeho!**
> **Glorify Him!"**

Then Tomasz's three brothers dashed to the bedroom door. The oldest brother blocked the doorway. The baby brother thought his oldest brother blocked the door so he could get out of the afghan and run down the steps with everyone. That was not the reason. Piotr held back the others to gain an advantage to be the first downstairs and, therefore, the first to open presents per the family tradition. The brothers rushed down the steps.

Untangled from the afghan, Tomasz sat on the edge of the bed and continued to compose himself. He could hear the oohs and aahs coming from the first-floor living room as his brothers surveyed what indeed was an overflowing pile of presents around the Christmas tree.

At that moment, Tomasz heard a noise over the loudness of the excitement from the living room. The noise was the pop of a tin top from the back bedroom.

Tomasz jerked—he was surprised by the sound. He quickly stood up and moved to the front bedroom doorway to make his way to the back bedroom. He stopped abruptly and thought, *What is going on here? Everyone is downstairs. Am I hearing things?*

Then, Tomasz heard the pop of a tin top being placed back on the can.

At the front bedroom doorway, Tomasz positioned himself to inch around the doorjamb to see who was in the back bedroom. As he inched around, he caught sight of a figure moving toward the back bedroom doorway.

Tomasz adjusted his stance and again inched around the jamb to better look at who was in the back bedroom. As he did, his eyes met his mother's eyes, and they both screamed and jumped back from surprise. As Mother jumped, some of the Kołaczki fell off the dish she was carrying.

"Tomasz, what are you doing up here?" Mother asked in a shaken tone from being surprised.

As Mother bent over to pick up the fallen cookies, she continued, "I thought all you boys were downstairs waiting for me to come down so you could start to open presents."

Mother stood up, and the cookies that fell off her plate were in her hand.

"Here," Mother said as she reached her hand out to her baby. "You can eat these three. They fell on the floor. I can't put them on the cookie tray. I'll eat these two."

Mother moved to the steps and started to descend as she continued her gleeful tone, "Come on. Hurry up. Let's go open presents."

"Okay, Mother. I want to put on a pair of socks. I'll be right down," Tomasz replied.

Tomasz turned and entered the front bedroom. He retrieved a pair of socks from his dresser and sat on a chair to put them on. He was again startled by a pop of a tin top from the back bedroom at that moment. He dropped his socks and sat straight up in the chair.

Tomasz thought, *This can't be happening. Did a tin top pop again? That's it! It may be too late to save the family, but that's it.*

This time, Tomasz immediately composed himself. He jumped from the chair, stuffed a nut-filled Kołaczki in his mouth and chewed as he quickly moved to the front bedroom doorway, through it, through the second doorway, and into the back bedroom. Then, barely in the room, he abruptly stopped from the scene that started to unfold.

Positioned by the wooden hope chest, standing next to the containers of Christmas Kołaczki, was a ghostly silhouette seemingly staring out the window. Then, the ghost slowly turned and faced Tomasz, and before his eyes, it morphed into an aged man with groomed dark hair parted on the right and combed straight down on the left, and a dark bushy mustache. He was dressed in a light gray suit, matching vest, white shirt, and complementing tie—the attire of the 1940s style. In his left hand, he cradled a handful of Christmas Kołaczki, in his right hand, a half-eaten Kołaczki.

Tomasz was startled by the now humanly figure. It was a striking likeness of the picture on the gravestone of Grandpa from Mine 40, Father's father. An image that stared out at Tomasz and his father as they cleaned the gravesite every Memorial Day holiday.

The figure raised his large left hand, opened it a bit, and showed off his extensive collection of Christmas Kołaczki. Then, with a giant smile on his face, he asked, "Do you like these, Tomasz?"

Tomasz said nothing; he was too shocked to reply. The resemblance to Grandpa from Mine 40 was almost too much. Nevertheless, Tomasz worked hard to keep his composure.

The ghostly figure sounded,

**Christos She Raghda!
Christ is born!**

**Proslavi Go!
Glorify Him!**

Then the ghost finished the Kołaczki from his right hand and continued, "Tomasz, don't worry about the old country curse, No Christmas Kołaczki. I've protected my baby boy and his family, and all the new country generations from the curse. So, everything is fine for now. You go and enjoy Christmas. But there are two things you have to do to help me keep the curse away."

Tomasz said nothing; he was still in a state of great surprise.

The ghost continued to sound, "Tomasz, you are my last grandson. You are my baby grandson like your mother calls you her baby boy. Like your father is my baby boy. But, as my last grandson, you must help me continue to protect the family.

You were given the middle name Michael, from Saint Michael the Archangel, the most powerful of the seven archangels. Michael is known as the greatest of all the angels. He works ceaselessly against the forces of darkness to bring about peace and harmony to all beings."

The ghostly figure paused and looked down as he reached his right hand to his left hand and fingered through his collection of Christmas **Kołaczki** until he picked a pineapple filling. He took a bite and slowly chewed. The ghost appeared to savor the taste.

When finished chewing, the figure sounded, "Tomasz, the first responsibility you have is to greet your mother and father with the Byzantine Christmas greeting in the Bulgarian language like I did to you. You must do it before opening presents, and you must do it for every Christmas to come. That is how you, with the middle name Michael, will continue to help me protect our family."

Tomasz started to feel a little comfortable with the presence of the ghost of Grandpa from Mine 40, and he replied, "I will. I will, Grandpa from Mine 40."

Again, the ghost of Grandpa from Mine 40 sounded,

"Your second responsibility. You will have grandsons and at least one will be given the middle name Michael. So, as I taught you how to help me, you must teach him and all your grandchildren how to fight the curse.

So, every Christmas morning, before opening presents, your grandchildren must greet their father and mother with the Byzantine Christmas greeting in Bulgarian. Like I did to you here. That is how you and your grandchildren will continue to help me protect our present and future families from the old country curse, No Christmas **Kołaczki**."

Before Grandpa from Mine 40 said anything else, Tomasz, with respect for his elders, dutifully replied, "Yes. Yes, I will, Grandpa from Mine 40."

With the instructions finalized and the recruitment concluded, the ghost of Grandpa from Mine 40 finished the second bite of the two-bite pineapple Kołaczki. Again, he delighted in the taste. After having enjoyed it, he floated to the wooden attic door, opened it, and drifted into the makeshift closet.

Grandpa from Mine 40 smiled large from inside the makeshift closet and said, "I'll see you again, Tomasz." Then, Tomasz witnessed the figure of Grandpa morph back to a ghostly silhouette as the wooden attic door slowly closed automatically.

Tomasz stood only a few steps into the back bedroom. He stood there and pondered the ghostly figure that had morphed to resemble the picture of Grandpa from Mine 40 on the gravestone and what the mysterious figure had said.

Tomasz stood in silence to absorb what had happened. Then he thought, *It must have been Grandpa from Mine 40; he was eating the Kołaczki. Father likes Kołaczki. The whole family likes Kołaczki. So, it had to be him. He was eating Kołaczki.*

Tomasz's thoughts were interrupted by his father's roar from the first-floor landing, "Tomasz, come on, we're waiting. Bring the small tin of Kołaczki down with you, too. Come on. Your brothers are waiting."

Cautiously, and keeping one eye on the closet door, Tomasz slowly moved to the wooden hope chest. He used two hands to pick up the small tin, pulled it into his chest, and hurried out of the back bedroom and down the steps. In the kitchen, he recklessly placed the container on the kitchen table.

Father gazed at Tomasz and said, "It looks like you saw a ghost."

Tomasz whispered, "Christos She Raghda!"

"What's that?" Father asked.

Tomasz spoke a little louder, "Christos She Raghda!"

Seated in his chair at the kitchen table, Father sat straight up. He finished a slow drag on his cigarette and held it for a couple of seconds. As he exhaled slower, he placed the cigarette in the ashtray slot to keep it burning. He looked hard at Tomasz and quietly responded,

"Proslavi Go!"

As Tomasz walked by his mother and father on his way to the living room to open presents with his brothers, he thought, *Will Father ask me questions? Will they believe what I have to say?*

"Hmm. I wonder where the baby learned that?" Mother asked. She was also seated at the kitchen table and eating Christmas **Kołaczki**.

Father said nothing. It seemed he knew and was content that the next generation was in control of the curse.

Mother moved from the kitchen table to the living room to be closer to the Christmas excitement from the opening of presents.

Father remained seated in his chair by the cellar door and watched his children open their Christmas gifts. He appeared to absorb their Christmas glee.

Busy with unwrapping presents, no one saw their stoic Father's brilliant blue eyes fill with tears. No one witnessed some of the tears drop to the rag rugs that covered the kitchen floor.

The End

LITERARY WORKS
BY
THOMAS SLATCOFF

Novels

Operation Red X
SLATCOFF AND COMPANY LLC, 2015

Atrocity in the Nave
SLATCOFF AND COMPANY LLC, 2017

The Respondent: A Person of Interest
SLATCOFF AND COMPANY LLC, 2019

Short Stories

The Respondent: A Person Bewitched
SLATCOFF AND COMPANY LLC,
2017 First eBook Edition
2022 First Soft Cover Print Edition

The Curse of No Christmas Kołaczki
SLATCOFF AND COMPANY LLC, 2021
2021 First eBook Edition
2022 First Soft Cover Print Edition
2022 First Hardcover Print Edition

Author Page
Amazon.com/author/ThomasSlatcoff

Let's stay in touch.

We trust you enjoyed the read and will want to enjoy other literary works by Thomas Slatcoff.

Please visit our website, **SLATCOFF.com**, for more information about the author, company, and products.

Don't miss new releases; use the below social media sites to stay connected and receive announcements of happenings and events.

THOMAS SLATCOFF

www.LinkedIn.com/In/ThomasSlatcoff

SLATCOFF AND COMPANY LLC

www.Facebook.com/SlatcoffandCompany

www.Twitter.com/SlatcoffandCo

Thomas can be reached at
Contact@Slatcoff.com

Made in the USA
Monee, IL
13 December 2022

8554b5fe-ca3d-4780-9680-509fdd0e5530R01